THE
SCIENCE FAIR
FROM THE
BLACK LAGOON

THE
SCIENCE FAIR
FROM THE
BLACK LAGOON

by Mike Thaler
Illustrated by Jared Lee

SCHOLASTIC INC.
New York   Toronto   London   Auckland   Sydney
Mexico City   New Delhi   Hong Kong   Buenos Aires

To Jarryd Hasfurther,
a hero of faith
—M.T.

To all those science geeks in the past
who make our lives easier today
—J.L.

ISBN 13: 978-0-439-55717-7
ISBN 10: 0-439-55717-8

Text copyright © 2004 by Mike Thaler.
Illustrations copyright © 2004 by Jared D. Lee Studio, Inc.

48 47 46 45 44 43 42 41 40 39 38   18 19 20

Printed in USA   40
This edition first printing, January 2009

CONTENTS

CHAPTER 1
IN THE BEGINNING

Mrs. Green says that we're going to have a science fair, and that we all have to invent something. I know all about inventors . . . I've seen them in the movies.

Inventors are a bunch of clowns with crazy hairdos, pop-bottle glasses, and baggy white coats. They are always trying to figure out ways to turn the world upside down!

Some inventors and scientists make monsters like *Dr. Franky Stein*. Some turn themselves into monsters like *Jacqueline Hyde*, who thought two heads were better than one.

What about *Dr. Buzz*? He turned himself into a giant fly. He was flying high until he got zapped by a S.W.A.T. team. Or *Dr. Dill*on, who turned himself into a giant pickle!

Then there are those scientists who just *grow* things in test tubes, like prime slime, glob blob, and muck yuck. They always get stuck late at the office and are totally absorbed in their work. I wonder if I'll get wrapped up in my invention.

SPLAT!

CHAPTER 2
INVENTION INTENTION

What will I invent?

When I get home, I put on my thinking cap. The wheel's been done. It's been *around* for years. And someone's had the bright idea to make the lightbulb. It's not fair. All the good inventions have been invented already.

Eric calls while I'm trying to figure it all out. He says he's going to make a Frankenstein monster. He wants to know whether I want to collect body parts with him.

I ask him where he's going to get them. He says that he's going to a body shop or a parts department. I tell him that I've got problems of my own, but I hope someone gives him a leg up, lends him a hand, or helps him get a*head*!

GLUE

HAIR

BANG
BANG
BANG

13

When I hang up, I'm still scratching my head. Then Derek calls. He says that he's going to make himself invisible.

"Outta sight!" I say.

"Yeah, I'll be able to get into the movies for free, steal lots of bases in Little League, and hang out in the teachers' lounge."

I tell him that I'll see him later.

I still don't have a clue what to do. Soon Doris calls and announces that she's going to win first prize with her invention. She tells me there have been oodles of great women scientists.

"Name one," I say.

"Madame Curious," she answers.

"What did she do?" I ask.

"She discovered radiators," Doris replies.

Then I ask Doris what her project is, and she asks me if I have security clearance. "I don't think so," I say. So she hangs up.

I'm still scratching my head when Freddy calls. He has a big-*time* idea. He's going to make a time machine and send himself into the future so he'll be old enough to drive.

Freddy also tells me that Penny is making a telescope and Randy is building a rocket.

I've got no idea what I'm going to do. Maybe I'll clone myself. Who knows?

19

CHAPTER 3

THE CLASS CLONE

If I had a clone, life would be twice as much fun. He could do my homework for me. He could get up early and go to school while I stayed in bed. He could do my chores around the house and always eat my broccoli and spinach at dinner.

He could even take my piano lesson and practice while I play baseball. Or he could be on my Little League team and help me make double plays. He could go to bed early while I stay up late. It would be great!

Plus, my clone could go to the dentist for me. He could get all my vaccinations and take my medicine when I get sick. Boy, if I had a clone, life would be twice as much fun . . . for me!

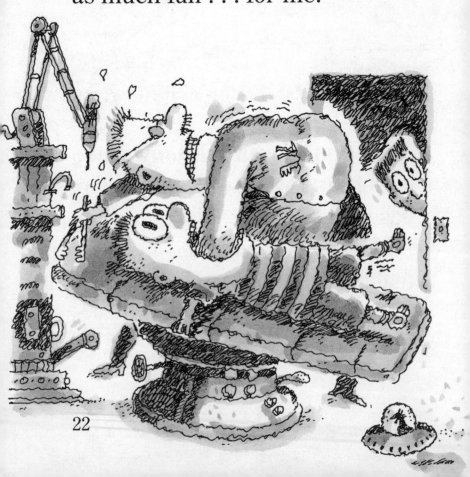

CHAPTER 4
DOCTOR BRAIN

I FEEL SMARTER ALREADY!

Mom asks me to take out the garbage. Where's my clone when I need him?

Then I have an idea. If I'm going to be a scientist, I have to look like one. So I mess up my hair—good start. I put on my trick glasses with the funny eyeballs—even better. Then I put on my mom's white coat—I'm there!

23

I look in the mirror and see a scientist looking back.

"Eureka! I've arrived!" I shout. There's a zingin' in my brain. Now I have lots of ideas!

I can make telephones out of two tin cans connected by a string. It would work for local calls. For long-distance calls, I'll just get a longer string.

I could make antigravity slippers out of banana peels, eyeballs out of eggshells, or roller skates out of apple cores.

Maybe I'll build a rocket, but that would make a lot of racket. I could create gum that quietly chews itself while you're in class! Or I could even make a TV remote that opens a book.

I could make a robot that rows a rowboat. I'll call him *Robert the Rowboat Robot.* It's a good tongue twister, anyway.

I'm too confused to choose. Cloning still leads the pack, but maybe I'll make a laugh machine.

ROW
ROW
ROW

CHAPTER 5
A SCI-FIVE

I turn on the TV and start watching the Sci Fi Channel. Mom tells me to do my homework. I tell her that I'm doing research!

There's a movie on called *Invasion of the Potty Snatchers*. It's about these Martians that come to Earth to steal all the toilets. I hope it has a happy ending.

At the end of the movie, the Martians flip their lids, learn to play kazoos, and join a Martian band. They wind up playing at halftime in the Super Bowl, where they're *flush*ed with excitement.

29

Next there's a movie about a mad scientist, *Dr. Midas.* Everything he touches turns to gold, so he runs for president, shakes a lot of hands, and becomes very rich. Unfortunately, he makes a bad investment when he picks his nose.

After that, there's another movie called *Eggs-tra Terrestrial*, about a hen-pecked husband who creates a giant chicken. Right before he takes over the world, he drowns in a large omelette. The police suspect *fowl* play.

Next there's *The Brainiac,* about a guy who turns ants into *gi*-ants. It's no picnic for him when they eat him out of house and home . . . and then eat him. He should have turned them into uncles.

Mom grabs the remote and beams me up to bed. If I only had my clone . . .

The next morning on the school bus, all the kids are talking about their science projects. Eric's down because he couldn't come up with one body part. No one lifted a *finger* to help him.

I can still see Derek, so he's not doing so well. Doris isn't talking much about her colossal invention. But Freddy says that he's making progress. He's one whole day into the future since yesterday.

Penny is still working on her telescope — with no end in sight. I tell her to get a movie magazine, where she's sure to see lots of stars. Randy's still trying to get his project off the ground.

WHICH END DO YOU LOOK THROUGH?

DAD'S LEAF BLOWER DOESN'T GIVE ME ENOUGH BOOST FOR BLAST OFF.

And I'm still undecided. It's between cloning myself and making a laugh machine. It's down to cloning or clowning!

CHAPTER 7

A BLAST FROM THE PAST

THE LIBRARIAN

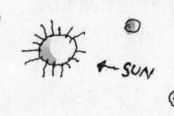

← SUN

← ONLY A CIRCLE

GALLEYOYO

In the library, Mrs. Beamster tells us about great scientists from the past. A guy named *Galleyoyo* said the earth was not the center of the universe. He made a lot of self-centered people mad.

← MOON

EARTH →

When Christopher Columbus said the earth was round, a lot of squares gave him a hard time.

Another guy named *Listermint,* made people angry when he told them to wash their hands to kill germs. I think that he was in *Germ*any. And a scientist named *Pasture* washed milk to get rid of *paris*ites. I think that he was from Paris.

GERMS

HOLD UP YOUR ARMS PLEASE.

 ← FIG

Another scientist named Newton was hit by a fig and invented the Fig Newton. *Ben Frankly* was shocked when everyone told him to go fly a kite. And Alexander Graham Bell invented graham crackers for your *belly*.

Mrs. Beamster says that everything we have today came from someone's imagination. And all the things we'll have tomorrow will come from ours. Boy, am I pumped!

CHAPTER 8
THE NAME GAME

I'm so excited! I check out a book called *How Inventions and Other Things Got Their Names*. It's very interesting. For instance, the guy who first ate an artichoke was named *Arty* and he *choked*.

The wheel was named because its inventor rode it down a hill and yelled, "Wheeee!" And his best friend said, "*We'll* have an awesome time with this."

Nomad scientists invented *sand*als for walking in the desert. They also invented *sand*paper and *sand*wiches.

Maybe I'll figure out an easy way to clone ice cream. And I'll call it—the ice-cream clone.

WHEEE!

SANDPAPER

SANDWICH

SANDY

SAND

WHICH ONE IS THE REAL ICE CREAM CONE?

Ⓐ Ⓑ

ANSWER ON PAGE 60.

43

CHAPTER 9
TOO MANY ME'S

CLONING

LAUGH MACHINE

WHICH SCIENCE PROJECT DO YOU THINK HUBIE SHOULD DO?

☆ CHOOSE ONE →

On the school bus ride home, I still can't decide whether I should clone myself or build a laugh machine. While I look out the bus window, I start to daydream about the science fair. But it's more like a *day-mare*!

I'm running on the playground. It's a bright, sunny day. I'm feeling good, but all of a sudden I bump into me.

"Why don't you look where I'm going?" I ask.

"Why don't you?" I reply.

We begin to argue, and a third me comes over to settle the fight, but he agrees with both of us. So we call over a fourth me. He's no help, either, and soon we're surrounded by a crowd of me's.

I ask, "Why don't we go play basketball?" But I can't seem to agree with myself.

Eleven me's want to play baseball, and I just want to wake up!

Suddenly, the bus horn honks and all the other me's vanish. I wipe my brow and decide not to clone myself. I look back into the window for a second opinion, but luckily I agree with me.

CHAPTER 10
GENIUS AT WORK

When I get off the bus, I go straight home from school and get to work. I realize that if I cloned myself, I would have to share my allowance. Bummer!

48

CHUCKLE!
CHUCKLE!
CHUCKLE!

So I'm going for the laugh machine. I mess up my hair, put on my crazy eyeball glasses, my white *laugh* coat, and go into my *laugh*ratory.

Maybe I'll just begin with a giggle machine or a chuckle box and work my way up. I squirt my dad's shaving cream on top of my head. I rub my mom's lipstick on the end of my nose. I look in the mirror and chuckle.

But when I go outside and show my dog, Tailspin, he just runs and hides. I show my mom, and she just tells me to go wash my face for dinner. Oh, well, back to the drawing board!

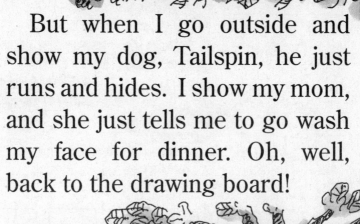

HUBIE, TIME FOR DINNER.

HOW DO I LOOK, MOM?

CHAPTER 11

A TOUGH ROW TO HO!

After dinner, I work late into the night. At 9:30 p.m., Mom tells me to go to bed. I still don't have my laugh machine finished, and tomorrow is the science fair.

When I fall asleep that night, I have a scream dream. It's the day of the fair. All the kids are in the gym with their projects.

Eric's monster is ten feet tall and sewn together. It looks like a cross between Coach Kong and Mrs. Beamster. It has a bolt in its neck and an outlet for its belly button. Eric tells it jokes to keep it in stitches.

I don't see Derek, but I guess that's a good sign. Doris's project is covered with a blanket and labeled TOP SECRET!

Penny's telescope looks like the one at the planetarium. I bet her father helped her. Randy's climbing aboard his rocket. And Freddy pulls the lever on his time machine. There's a *pop, bop,* and *boom!* When the smoke clears, we're all standing in the future.

Freddy has a beard and is old enough to drive, but there are no more cars. In fact, there are no more streets, just sidewalks everywhere. Bummer!

There was just too much pollution, so now everyone has to walk. There's a walk-through fast-food place, a walk-by bank, and walk-in movie theaters. Even NASCAR is *NASWALK*.

Freddy is sad. I guess now it's

time for my laugh machine. I wind it up and it says, "Ho, ho, ho!" But no one else is laughing. They all just walk away.

I wake up and roll out of bed. It's Saturday—time for the science fair.

CHAPTER 12
BRAINSTORM!

While I'm brushing my teeth, I suddenly have it! Yes! It will work. I high-five the mirror and get to work.

By 11:00 a.m., I'm putting on the finishing touches. I print LAUGH MACHINE on my T-shirt. The science fair is at 1:00 p.m. I put on my backpack and I'm ready to roll.

I sit in the van and feel like I'm driving into the future. If I win first prize at the science fair, I'll go on to become a famous *fizzy*-cist and invent lots of neat stuff.

And my best invention will be my *Lazy-ier Ray*. When people get excited and want to fight, I'll zap them with my *Lazy-ier Ray* and they'll just yawn and go back to bed. I'll call it the *Have-A-Nice-Day Ray* and I will win the *No Bell Pizza Prize*.

We pull up at school. I get out of the van and walk into the gym with confidence.

CHAPTER 13
OUR INVENTION CONVENTION

All the kids are standing by their projects. There are lots of cool things to see. I hope people like my laugh machine.

Instead of Frankenstein, Eric brought in his dog, Butch, who has a bolt in his collar.

I see Derek is not invisible, but he's handing out blindfolds to everyone. "Put them on," he smiles. We do. "Now can you see me?" he asks.

"No," we answer.

"Eureka!" he shouts.

Penny has taped together ten toilet paper tubes and hung a paper star on the end.

SCIENCE FAIR TODAY →

Randy pushes a button and his rocket falls over. "It's *rocket roll*," he says.

Freddy has a sign that his time machine is in the future and won't be back until tomorrow.

And Doris still isn't showing her project to anybody.

ANSWER: (A)

I guess it's time for my laugh machine. I turn around and open my backpack. I put on my googly eyes, my vampire fangs, my picnic plate ears, and my propeller beanie. I twirl my propeller, stick my finger in my nose, spin around three times, cross my eyes, press my belly button and . . . burp!

BURP!

HA 62 HA HA HA HA HA HA HA

Everyone laughs, even Mrs. Green. She awards me a special prize for the "Silliest Invention."

Hey, science is a blast! Maybe next year we'll have our science fair on the moon, and I'll be an astro-*nut!*